WORLD CULTURES

INUIT

LESLIE STRUDWICK

MEDIA ENHANCED BOOKS
AV2
BY WEIGL™
ADDED VALUE • AUDIO VISUAL

www.av2books.com

AV² provides enriched content that supplements and complements this book. Weigl's AV² books strive to create inspired learning and engage young minds in a total learning experience.

Your AV² Media Enhanced books come alive with...

Audio
Listen to sections of the book read aloud.

Key Words
Study vocabulary, and complete a matching word activity.

Video
Watch informative video clips.

Quizzes
Test your knowledge.

Embedded Weblinks
Gain additional information for research.

Slide Show
View images and captions, and prepare a presentation.

Try This!
Complete activities and hands-on experiments.

... and much, much more!

Go to **www.av2books.com**, and enter this book's unique code.

BOOK CODE

N 7 6 9 8 2 8

AV² by Weigl brings you media enhanced books that support active learning.

Published by AV² by Weigl
350 5ᵗʰ Avenue, 59ᵗʰ Floor
New York, NY 10118
Website: www.av2books.com   www.weigl.com

Library of Congress Cataloging-in-Publication Data

Strudwick, Leslie, 1970-
 Inuit / Leslie Strudwick.
   p. cm. -- (World cultures)
 Includes index.
 ISBN 978-1-61913-092-0 (hard cover : alk. paper) -- ISBN 978-1-61913-530-7 (soft cover : alk. paper)
 1. Inuit--Juvenile literature. I. Title.
 E99.E7S8375 2012
 979.8004'9712--dc23

                    2011051109

Printed in the United States of America in North Mankato, Minnesota
1 2 3 4 5 6 7 8 9 0 16 15 14 13 12

062012
WEP170512

Senior Editor Heather Kissock
Art Director Terry Paulhus

Photo Credits
Every reasonable effort has been made to trace ownership and to obtain permission to reprint copyright material. The publishers would be pleased to have any errors or omissions brought to their attention so that they may be corrected in subsequent printings.

Weigl acknowledges Getty Images and Alamy as primary photo suppliers for this title.

CONTENTS

Where in the World?

PACIFIC OCEAN

UNITED STATES (ALASKA)

CANADA

ARCTIC OCEAN

RUSSIA

GREENLAND

ATLANTIC OCEAN

LEGEND
■ Inuit Distribution

PACIFIC OCEAN

ARCTIC OCEAN

ATLANTIC OCEAN

**Indigenous Population
(Inuit):** more than 160,000

Region: Arctic

Continents: Asia,
North America

**Countries Where Inuit
Live:** Canada, Greenland,
Russia, United States

The area that surrounds the North Pole where the ground stays frozen throughout the entire year is called the **Arctic**. **Inuit** live in the Arctic areas of Canada, Greenland, Russia, and the United States. Though Inuit communities are located across the Arctic landscape, most Inuit live near water.

About 5,000 to 10,000 years ago, groups of people traveled from Asia to North America. It is believed that they crossed the Pacific Ocean using the Bering Land Bridge. Large glaciers that covered much of North America and northern Europe had not yet melted. Sea levels were lower, exposing a large area of land. This Bering Land Bridge created a passage between Siberia and Alaska. During a hunt, **ancestors** of the Inuit followed herds of animals across the land bridge. This first group of peoples settled in the Alaska region. About 4,000 years ago, the **climate** warmed. These peoples, known as the Pre-Dorset culture, started to move farther east. The Pre-Dorset peoples carved tools from antlers, ivory, bone, and stone, and used **harpoons** to hunt.

The Pre-Dorset culture **evolved** over a period of 3,000 years. They became the Dorset peoples. The Dorset lived in communities of three to 15 families. In the summer, they lived in tents made of animal skins. In the winter, they built homes partially underground. These peoples were skilled artists. Sculptures found in the area suggest the Dorset peoples carved Arctic animals, such as birds, polar bears, and seals. The Dorset believed some of these carvings were magical.

About 1,000 years ago, early Inuit peoples from Alaska spread across the Arctic. One group, known as the Thule, traveled as far as northeastern Greenland. The Thule mainly used the bowhead whale for food and tools. Their **descendants** are the Inuit of today. Modern Inuit culture evolved around 1750.

For decades, the **indigenous peoples** of the Arctic were called "Eskimos." The Ojibwa Native Peoples gave them this name, which was thought to mean "eater of raw meat." **Linguists** now believe the word Eskimo means "to net snowshoes." The word Inuit, which means "the people," was made the official name of the Arctic peoples in 1977. Inuit is the word used to describe the entire group of these indigenous peoples. One member of the group is called an Inuk.

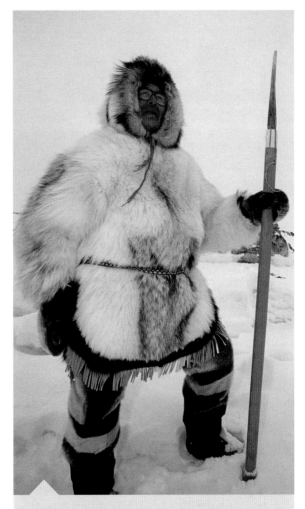

In the Arctic, there are very few resources available to make tools and weapons. The Inuit used walrus tusks and antlers to make useful weapons, such as harpoons.

Culture Cues

🐾 Husky dogs are used to pull sleds in the Arctic because they are strong and can pull heavy loads over long distances. These dogs have thick fur coats, and they prefer living in cool climates.

🐾 The average summer temperature in the Arctic is 50° Fahrenheit (10° Celsius).

🐾 Before 1867, Alaska was part of Russia. It became part of the United States that year.

🐾 More than 400 types of flowering plants grow in the Arctic.

Stories and Legends

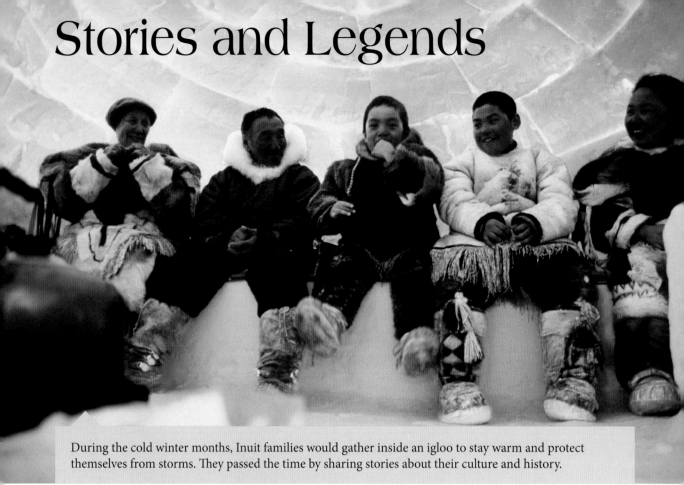

During the cold winter months, Inuit families would gather inside an igloo to stay warm and protect themselves from storms. They passed the time by sharing stories about their culture and history.

Creating and telling stories was an important part of Inuit culture. During the cold days and long nights of the winter months, the Inuit spent much time inside. Families and communities would share stories to entertain each other. They often used songs to tell stories. The songs explained a story or described an event. Dancing was also used to tell some stories.

Inuit storytelling taught values and proper ways of doing things. It was also a way to pass Inuit history along to young people. Elders would tell stories to their children and grandchildren. Storytelling was a fun game for children. Most girls were given carved "storyknives" from their fathers. The girls used these knives to draw pictures in the ground as they told their stories. They told tales about their families, animals, and nature.

Drum dancing was an important part of most gatherings. These dances were performed to celebrate births, successful hunts, and the changing of the seasons.

Like most other cultures, the Inuit used legends to explain the creation of the world. They also told stories of spirits who watched over their people. For example, they believed that the **Northern Lights** were the souls of their ancestors playing kickball. They also believed that these lights were torches held by ancient ancestors to light a path for the souls of the dead.

One legend tells of the man who created the world. He built himself wings, and a sparrow taught him how to fly. This man became a raven. With the sparrow's help, the raven created other people from clay. He also created animals for the people to hunt. To create night and day, the raven threw light and dark rocks into the sky.

Another story describes the creation of day and night. In this story, the Sun is a spirit girl who carries a torch. The Moon is her older brother. He is a good hunter. Day and night come as the Moon chases the Sun across the sky. The torch flickers as he tries to grab it away from his sister.

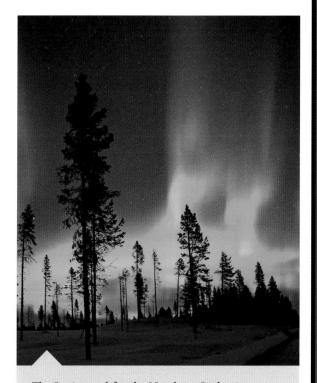

The Inuit word for the Northern Lights is *arsaniit*, which means "the kickball game."

THE STORY OF
Sedna, the Inuit Goddess of the Sea

In one version of an Inuit legend, Sedna believed she was too beautiful to marry just anyone. One day, a man wearing a dark hood offered her happiness. She agreed to marry him.

The man took Sedna to his home. It was a nest on a cliff. He took down his hood to reveal that he was a raven. He fed Sedna raw fish. Sedna was very unhappy. She called out for her father to rescue her. He arrived one year later, and they paddled away in his boat. The raven chased behind.

To lose the bird, Sedna's father tossed Sedna into the ocean. She clung to the boat, but her father hit her fingers with his paddle. Her fingers broke off and sank into the ocean. Her fingers became ocean animals.

Today, Sedna is the goddess of the sea. She sends seals and whales to the Inuit. When the Inuit have done something bad, she withholds her animals to punish them.

Out of the Past

Life has always been difficult for the indigenous peoples of the Arctic region. The climate has always been rugged and harsh. The Inuit, and their ancestors, have had to work hard to survive. Still, they greatly enjoy life.

Over the past 10,000 years, there have been times when the climate warmed. During these times, Inuit ancestors were able to move farther east from Alaska. Warming trends meant that more animals were available to hunt. Warm summer months allowed for a longer growing season. As a result, there were more berries to pick. When the climate cooled again, food sources were harder to find. With the lack of food, whole communities disappeared.

The Arctic climate has not changed much since the arrival of the Europeans in the 1500s. The Europeans discovered Inuit settlements while searching for a shorter route from the Atlantic Ocean to the Pacific Ocean. Before their arrival, the Inuit did not have much contact with different cultures other than neighboring Native groups. The arrival of the Europeans changed their lives.

Timeline of the Inuit

1500s European explorers have their first encounter with Inuit communities.

1610 While searching for the Northwest Passage, Henry Hudson reaches the mouth of the Hudson River.

5,000 years ago The Pre-Dorset peoples move east from the Bering Land Bridge, building communities in the Arctic regions.

10,000 years ago A group of people travel from Asia to North America across the Bering Land Bridge.

Many of the items the Europeans brought to the Arctic were useful. The Inuit traded furs and oil for food, guns, and supplies. Guns made hunting easier, but they also caused some changes to Inuit culture.

As a result of European settlement in the Arctic, the Inuit spent more time trapping furs to trade, which meant they spent more time hunting and less time finding food. Fewer Inuit were living the traditional **nomadic** lifestyle. Governments were established in the North, and settlements were built near trading posts. These settlements included houses, nursing stations, and schools. Soon, many Inuit traded for the items they needed for their daily lives.

Along with fur traders came missionaries. Missionaries are people who spread their religion to other cultures. Sometimes, they believe they are creating a better living situation for these cultures. Although the missionaries believed they were helping the Inuit, they were actually changing the way the Inuit lived. The Inuit's traditional **spiritual** beliefs started to fade as they learned more about European culture.

Early 1700s Whaling begins in the Arctic.

1903 The first Royal Canadian Mounted Police posts are established to maintain law and order throughout the North.

1771 The first missionaries arrive in the Canadian Arctic. They settle in the village of Nain and form a mission station.

Late 1800s **Commercial** whaling stops. **Overharvesting** of whales has left too few whales in Arctic waters.

April 1, 1999 Nunavut becomes the third Canadian territory. The territory is dedicated to **preserving** the Inuit culture.

Social Structures

Family has always been very important to the Inuit. Groups of hunting families lived and worked together to increase their chances of finding and sharing food. Each person's role was equally important. In Inuit society, the roles of men and women were strictly defined. The men fished, hunted, and built houses. The women tanned animal skins and dried meat after a hunt. Women also cooked and sewed clothing. Children were always expected to help. Boys helped at home until they could hunt, and girls worked with their mothers.

Inuit groups moved from place to place throughout the year. The group camped for a few months in places where there were many animals to hunt. Each group was much like one big family. They functioned without government, tribes, and chiefs. Although some people acted as leaders, they did not tell other group members what to do. Instead, they listened to people and offered advice. These leaders were often the oldest members of the group.

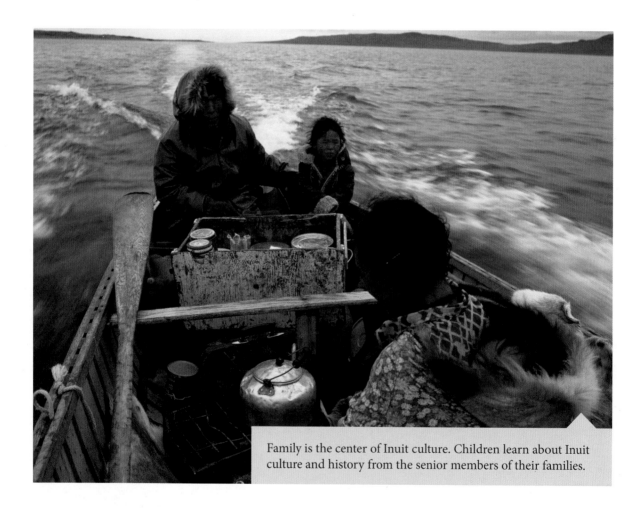

Family is the center of Inuit culture. Children learn about Inuit culture and history from the senior members of their families.

Today, an Inuit shaman may teach others about the spiritual life and customs of his or her people.

A spiritual leader, or shaman, was part of most communities. The shaman was an advisor and doctor. The shaman was also able to talk to spirits. A shaman could be either a man or a woman.

It was believed that people were born with the gift to see spirits and visions. A shaman was one who improved these gifts through years of training. To heal or help answer questions, the shaman spent long periods of time away from the community and performed rituals that involved singing, dancing, and drumming.

Families in a community shared everything. When a large animal was killed, the food was divided so that every family had a portion. Today, many Inuit families do not hunt for survival. Family is still an important part of the Inuit culture, however. For example, grandparents help raise the children.

THE TWO SEASONS

During the summer months, the Sun never sets in the Arctic. The land is covered with many flowering plants. During the winter months, the Sun does not rise for many weeks, or even months, depending on the region. The winter climate is bitterly cold, with heavy snowfalls and harsh winds.

Communication

Oral, or spoken, language was the most important form of communication for the Inuit. They have always used the spoken word to teach their culture and traditions to younger members of the community. Writing is a fairly new form of communication for the Inuit. Before missionaries arrived in the Arctic, the Inuit did not have a written language. There was no need to write. Living in such small groups, it was easy to share stories using just the spoken word. Children learned everything they needed to know from their parents and other adults. Ideas of right and wrong were taught through oral stories.

The Inuit began writing in Inuktitut about 100 years ago. Missionaries created a writing system using the Inuit language. The Inuit used this writing system, called "syllabics," to record traditions and beliefs. In some Arctic regions, the English, or Roman, alphabet is used.

There are different **dialects** of Inuktitut, but each is a variation of the same language. While some senior Inuit peoples may only speak Inuktitut, most of their children speak English as well. Some children only speak English, but many Inuit communities work to preserve their language by teaching it in school.

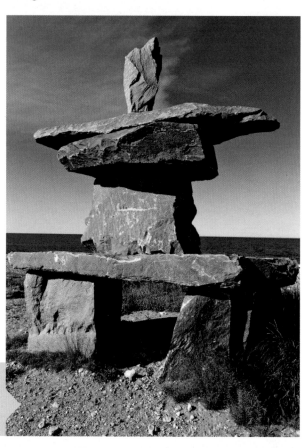

The Inuit built tall, stone markers called *Inukshuk* to help guide them across the land. Inukshuk means "like a person."

INUKTITUT

When a writing system was first introduced to the Inuit more than 100 years ago, words were spelled the way they sounded. This caused the same word to be spelled many different ways. For example, people of European descent are both *qallunaaq* and *kabloona*.

Although both words are spelled differently, they are pronounced almost the same way.

Since the mid-1970s, the Inuit have tried to **standardize** the language.

As other cultures introduced new objects to the Inuit, they created Inuktitut words for these items. For example, before European whalers arrived in the North, the Inuit did not have tea or sugar. They created the word *tii* for "*tea*," and *sukaq* for "*sugar*." More words were created when fur traders settled in the Arctic and the Inuit were introduced to spoons, kettles, and many other items.

Some cultures believe that the Inuit have 100 different ways to say the word "snow." This is not true. There is one Inuktitut word for snow: *aput*. Similar to the English language, there are many Inuktitut words to describe different types of snow. For example, "fluffy," "slush," and "sticky" are some of the words to describe snow.

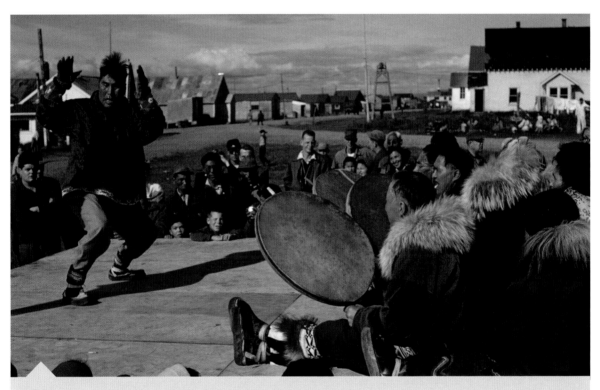

Dancing is a traditional way for the Inuit to communicate with each other and the spirit world. Drum dancing is still performed at gatherings and celebrations.

Law and Order

Traditional Inuit societies followed formal laws. The Inuit knew that the best way to stay alive was to always act in the best interest of the group. This helped to keep peace. The Inuit believed spirits would judge a person's behavior and punish any wrongdoing. They thought that everything had a soul. If the soul was mistreated, its spirit would return from the dead to get revenge.

Rather than written laws, the Inuit had specific rules, or principles. Since the Inuit believed animals had souls, they had respect for the animals they hunted. They treated animals with care even after the kill. They refused to hunt land and sea animals using the same weapons. If an animal was killed on land, it was cooked on land. To prevent upsetting caribou spirits, it was forbidden for dogs to eat their bones on the site where the animal was killed. Since both wolves and bears were dangerous to hunt, special offerings were made to their spirits after a kill. The Inuit feared that the spirits might punish them with starvation if they did not treat the animals well.

All members of the group obeyed hunting customs. It was believed that they would suffer nature's revenge if these customs were ignored. For example, if the customs were not followed, the group believed hunts would

Traditionally, the Inuit have very strict rules for hunting to preserve game for future generations. These rules ensure that all animals are treated with respect.

be unsuccessful, or stormy weather would make it hard for them to hunt.

While a few communities still follow these early customs, most Inuit follow different rules today. They follow the laws of the country in which they live. However, some countries recognize that Inuit laws may be more suitable than modern laws. Punishment in some Inuit communities may be different than those in large, modern cities. For example, three boys in a Canadian Inuit community attacked and injured a man. These boys were not jailed. Instead, they were **banished** to an island where no other

people lived. They had to find a way to live—much like their ancestors did when they first settled in the Arctic. This was hard for the boys since they were raised in communities that had fridges, stoves, televisions, and other modern items.

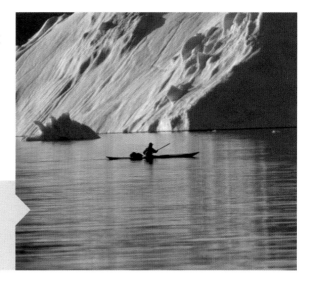

Some Inuit offenders are given traditional sentences, such as banishment, instead of being sent to jail. People found guilty of a crime are taken to isolated areas where they are expected to live off the land.

Celebrating Culture

Inuit culture includes art, dance, and song. Inuit culture is also present in the way these indigenous peoples live. This includes their physical skills, the games they play, the foods they eat, and the clothing they wear. Inuit peoples believe the Arctic animals, land, sea, and weather are also part of their culture. They use the word *illiquusiq*, which means "ways and habits," to refer to their culture and way of life.

Since Inuit culture cannot be separated from the environment, the Inuit respect their surroundings. Animals are part of their culture, so they treat them with respect. The Inuit believe that animals are on Earth to provide food and clothing for their survival. To show their respect, the Inuit only hunt as many animals as they need. All parts of an animal are used, so its life is not wasted.

Music, singing, and dancing often play a part in Inuit celebrations such as a marriage or the birth of a child.

The Inuit express their culture through the games they play and by wearing traditional clothing made of animal skins.

Over the past 100 years, Inuit culture has changed, but many of the cultural beliefs remain the same. Although they live in houses and shop in stores for food, many Inuit still take part in hunting trips. They build igloos to live in while they are on the hunt. The Inuit now use rifles as well as harpoons for hunting animals.

The Inuit continue to respect the animals that they hunt for food. They celebrate family as the core of Inuit culture. Like their ancestors, they tell stories to teach a lesson, sing to tell of a great adventure, dance to celebrate a successful hunt, and play games to bring their communities together.

Today, the Inuit use modern tools for hunting animals. However, they remain linked to their traditions.

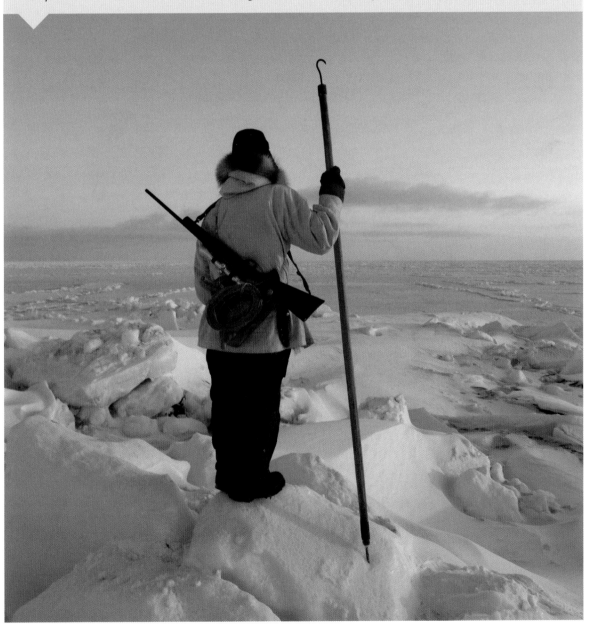

Art and Culture

Inuit sculptures are well-known in many parts of the world. Sculpting skills were first developed thousands of years ago when the Inuit made tools and weapons from antlers, bones, or walrus tusks. In addition to tools, they made toys and small figures for children. At first, they carved practical objects for their own families, such as combs and needle cases. Once the Europeans arrived, the Inuit traded these objects for other items.

Inuit sculptures were brought to other cultures after a young, Canadian art student named James Houston visited the Arctic in 1948. He brought some Inuit carvings to Canadian museums and stores. Houston asked the Inuit to make more carvings in exchange for flour, pots, and tobacco. Soon, people around the world wanted to buy these beautiful works of art. Some Inuit artists were able to earn a living creating works from antlers, bone, ivory, and stone.

Many Inuit artists make their living by selling their art. Each year, the Inuit Art Society meets to support the culture and help educate the public about Inuit art.

Inuit peoples used clothing to display their art. Inuit women often decorated their clothing with colored fur and feathers to make different patterns. They sewed small pieces of bone, ivory, or shells to form shapes on clothes. They also used some of these items to make jewelry. Today, Inuit art is displayed and sold in many countries around the world.

More recently, Inuit artists have started to make prints and paint. They carve images of animals, people, spirits, and mythological figures into stone. These images are covered in paint and pressed onto paper. The Inuit also paint on **canvas**. They often use their artwork to show their respect for animals and nature. Today, some villages earn their entire income by selling Inuit art.

Some Inuit dress in highly decorated clothing for celebrations.

Carving in Stone

Soapstone was once the most common stone used for Inuit art. Soapstone is soft and easy to carve, but it is sturdy. Today, many Inuit carve their art in a stone called serpentine. Serpentine is similar to soapstone, but it breaks less easily. Most stone is collected from a quarry near an artist's community. Often, it is possible to determine which community produced a piece of art based on the type of stone that was used.

Dressing Up

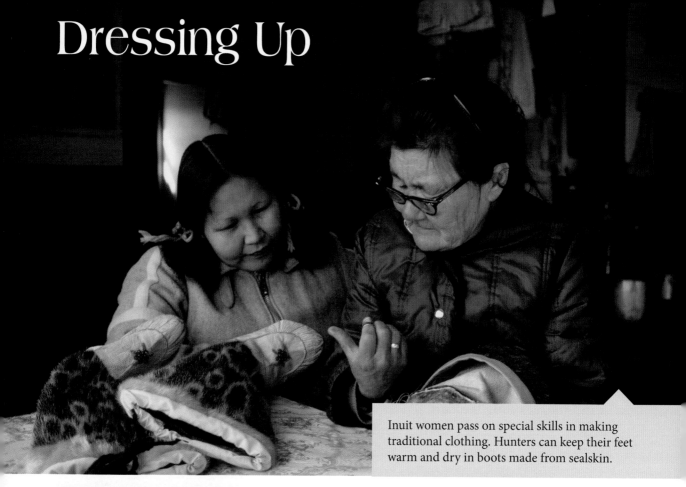

Inuit women pass on special skills in making traditional clothing. Hunters can keep their feet warm and dry in boots made from sealskin.

Winter parkas are usually made of caribou or polar bear skin.

The Inuit could not have lived in the Arctic without proper clothing. They needed warm, waterproof clothing to keep warm in the chilly and windy Arctic climate.

Inuit women made clothes from animal skins and furs. Some clothing items were made from caribou **hide**. Women also used bird feathers, or fox, polar bear, and wolf furs, to make warm clothing.

Inuit usually wore a long, heavy fur coat called a parka. They also wore boots, mittens, and pants. On very cold days, they wore two layers of clothing. Body heat became trapped in the air between the layers, keeping the wearer warmer. During the summer months, lightweight, waterproof clothes were made from sealskin. From head to toe, a winter outfit could weigh as much as 10 pounds (4.5 kilograms).

While women's and men's clothes were very similar, there were a few differences. Women in Greenland wore thigh-high boots, which were lined with moss or dried grass. Men wore shorter boots. Women often wore parkas that had a fur-lined pouch called an *amautik*. They used this pouch to carry their babies on their back.

Women worked hard to make clothes for their family. An animal hide was stretched and dried before it was scraped clean. To soften the hide, women chewed it with their front teeth. Chewing also helped to waterproof the hide. They sewed the seams tightly to keep out wind and cold weather. **Narwhal sinews**, or those from the beluga whale, were often used as thread.

Although some clothing items are still made using traditional methods, most Inuit peoples buy their clothes from stores. Furs and hides are still worn to keep hunters warm during long trips.

Women prepared animal hides to make clothing.

FEET FIRST

Traditional boots, or *kamiit*, are made from seal or caribou skins. At one time, kamiit were an important part of the Inuit wardrobe. They prevented injuries that can be caused by exposure to snow and cold temperatures.

In order to keep their feet from freezing during harsh winter weather, hunters wore kamiit made from shaved sealskin or haired caribou skin. Kamiit were waterproof and provided protection in wet regions. Haired sealskin or caribou hide kamiit were worn during cold, dry, winter weather.

Food and Fun

It was difficult to find food in the Arctic. The weather was too cold to grow crops, so the Inuit hunted animals as their main source of food. Hunting skills have kept the Inuit way of life alive for thousands of years. Depending on the time of year, the Inuit hunted different animals. When the ice melted in the summer months, they hunted birds, fish, seals, walruses, and whales. During the warmer months, they also picked berries and dug plant roots from the ground. In the colder months, the Inuit hunted caribou, seals, and sometimes polar bears. The Inuit called these traditional food sources "country food."

The Inuit peoples often ate raw meat. Raw food did not take much time to prepare. Raw meat also had more vitamins than cooked meat, and it was healthier for their diet. Since fruits and vegetables did not grow in the Arctic, the Inuit ate raw meat to get the vitamins they needed to stay healthy. They would dry some of the fish they caught in the summer, so it could be eaten during the winter months. Sometimes, meat was cut into small pieces and dipped in salt.

Inuit Diet

Cranberries

Whales

Caribou

Polar bears

Salmon

Seals

Blueberries

Inuit traditionally ate mostly seafood and red meat.

Fruits
Seafood
Red Meat

Traditional Inuit games, such as sky tossing, are still enjoyed by communities today.

To the Inuit, preparing meals and eating with friends and family was a fun activity. They thought food tasted better when it was shared, so communities ate together.

Laughing and playing was a welcome change from hunting and working. Many Inuit children and adults played games, such as sky tossing, which was the first form of trampoline. To play, one person stood in the center of a large, circular piece of animal hide. Many other people stood around the hide, holding the edges. As they pulled the edges, the person standing in the center of the hide was tossed into the air. Other games, such as arm pulling, kickball or *aqsaq*, high kicks, seal-hop, and tag required the players to use their hunting skills. Many of these games did not need equipment. Instead, they required strength and **agility**.

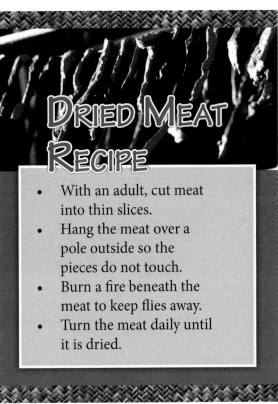

DRIED MEAT RECIPE

- With an adult, cut meat into thin slices.
- Hang the meat over a pole outside so the pieces do not touch.
- Burn a fire beneath the meat to keep flies away.
- Turn the meat daily until it is dried.

Great Ideas

There are not many building materials in the Arctic. Since trees were not available for lumber, the Inuit used snow to build their houses. Many people call these houses igloos, but the Inuit call them *igluigaq*, which means "snow house." *Iglu* is the Inuktitut word for "house."

To build an igloo, the Inuit would cut, or saw, large blocks of packed snow. They piled these blocks on top of one another in the shape of a spiral. This formed a **dome**. They filled the cracks between the blocks with snow. A low, short tunnel was built on one side of the dome. This tunnel was used as a doorway. The tunnel kept cold air from blowing into the dome. Often, a cold trap, or sunken area, was cut inside the tunnel. Inside, the igloo was covered with warm furs. Igloos were usually used as temporary homes during winter hunting trips. Summer homes were built from sod or grass. Tents were built using **driftwood** and whalebones as poles and seal or caribou skins as coverings.

Dogsleds and **kayaks** helped the Inuit travel far distances for hunting. Walking was especially slow in the winter when people had to trek through

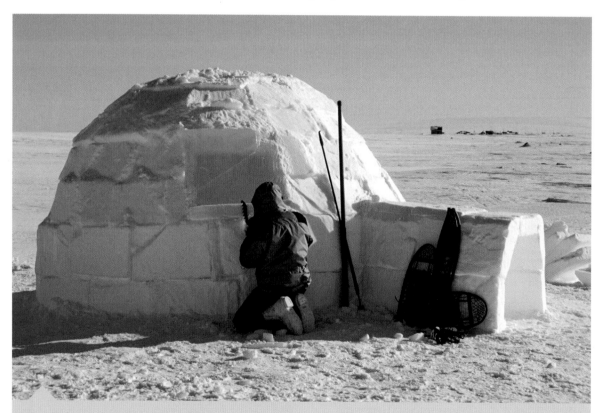

Inuit peoples no longer live in igloos. Still, igloos are sometimes used as shelter for hunters and travelers in the Far North where there are no trees to build tents.

A sled dog team can pull a load weighing hundreds of pounds (kilograms). Sled dogs have a heavy coat that allows them to withstand the severe cold.

deep snow wearing heavy clothing. A team of dogs could pull a sled loaded with supplies, meat, and even a few people.

Kayaks were built to fit a single rider. Made from a wooden frame and covered with seal skin, a kayak could move easily through water. It was important for kayaks to move quickly and turn easily when the Inuit were hunting large fish and whales. Several hunters would work together to catch a whale. On hunting trips, they used larger boats called *umiaks* to carry children, women, and supplies.

The Hunting Boat

The Inuit used kayaks to glide through the water and hunt sea mammals. A kayak looked like a narrow canoe with a deck where harpoons could be stored. It had a wood frame that came to a point at both ends. It was covered with seal or caribou skin. The paddler sat in a small opening in the deck of the kayak. He wore a special jacket made of seal **intestine**. This jacket was fitted around the edge of the opening to create a waterproof seal. To move the boat through the water, the paddler used a long paddle with a blade at each end,

or a short paddle with a blade on one end. If the kayak tipped, the paddler could use the paddle to right the boat and continue the hunt.

At Issue

Today, most Inuit live in modern homes in settled communities.

Many ancient Inuit customs are gradually disappearing. Most Inuit peoples no longer move from one place to another in search of food. Instead, they live in settled communities. Like many modern societies, they shop at grocery stores, buy clothes, and watch television.

Though many Inuit peoples no longer hunt full-time, they still follow some of their ancient hunting traditions. However, pollution from southern regions has poisoned some of the Inuit's hunting grounds and harmed many animals. Some fish and whales may not be safe to eat.

While the Inuit have killed seals for hundreds of years and used their skins to make clothes and food, today many people do not believe animals should be killed for their fur. The Inuit once ate seal meat and sold extra skins for money. Many Inuit groups depended on the money they earned trading furs and skins. Now, very few people will buy animal skins. Many Inuit communities have stopped practicing their ancient traditions. They no longer trade for food and other items. Instead, they use money to buy items such as blue jeans and T-shirts, canned or packaged foods, televisions, and electricity.

Self-government is another topic at issue for Inuit peoples. Before the Arctic regions became part of the United States, Canada, Greenland, and Russia, the Inuit lived by their own rules. However, other countries have claimed these regions, and the Inuit are expected to obey the national laws of these countries.

These laws do not always work well for Inuit communities. The Inuit would rather have their own laws and government tailored to their unique way of life.

In 1999, a new territory was created in Canada. This territory is named Nunavut, which means "our land" in Inuktitut. Most of the people living in Nunavut are Inuit. In Nunavut, Inuit work in the government to preserve Inuit traditions and create a governing system that suits the needs of their peoples. Inuktitut is the official language of Nunavut. However, **interpreters** translate in multiple languages for members of the Nunavut legislature. English, Inuktitut, and French are the most common languages.

Inuit Circumpolar Conference

In June 1977, the Inuit Circumpolar Conference (ICC) was formed to protect the interests of indigenous Arctic peoples. Inuit representatives from Alaska, Canada, and Greenland gathered in Barrow, Alaska, to determine how they could protect the culture, rights, and traditions of the Arctic peoples.

The ICC General Assembly is held every four years. Inuit from the Arctic regions, including Russia, gather to elect a president and **council**. During this meeting, they discuss issues regarding their rights and culture. They also establish ways to maintain Inuit culture and identity.

Into the Future

Most Inuit communities have a village or hamlet council that makes laws for the residents. Since there are very few jobs in the Arctic, people must work together as a community to survive. The local council manages community **finances**. In each community, a cooperative board of directors operates stores and exports artwork, fish, furs, handmade crafts, and pelts.

Stores in Inuit villages bring modern goods and products to people. Many people want the items they see advertised on television and online. These communities are also connected to the rest of the world. Airplanes, boats, buses, cars, the internet, and roads all serve to connect people living in the Arctic to other regions. While some Inuit may still prefer to live following the traditions of their ancestors, it is not always an option. Some of the animals they once hunted for food are now **endangered**, and it is illegal to kill them. Chemicals spilled in Arctic waters have poisoned other animals.

Most Inuit children no longer help their mothers sew or prepare food and skins, nor do they help their fathers hunt every day. Instead, they go to school. Arctic schools teach Inuit children about their history and traditions. Children learn traditional stories and are taught to speak Inuktitut. Students learn traditional skills such as building wooden sleds and sewing skins. They also learn about Inuit art and culture.

Some Inuit peoples have become famous outside of their communities. Susan Aglukark is a popular singer in Canada and Alaska. She sings in both English and Inuktitut. Songs such as *O Siem* and *Hina Na Ho* tell stories about the Inuit and the issues facing them. "O Siem" is an expression of joy used by Inuit peoples to greet friends and family. *Hina Na Ho* is a song about surviving a cold, Arctic winter.

Kenojuak Ashevak is a well-known Inuit artist. She paints, does beadwork, draws, and carves. Born in 1927, Ashevak lived a traditional nomadic Inuit life. In 1963, the National Film Board of Canada made a film about her to document Inuit art. Although her work is sold in stores around the world, she continues to live in her Inuit community.

In school, Inuit children learn the language and traditions of their people.

Role-play Debate

When people debate a topic, two sides take a different viewpoint about one idea. Each side presents logical arguments to support its views. In a role-play debate, participants act out the roles of the key people or groups involved with the different viewpoints. Role-playing can build communication skills and help people understand how others may think and feel. Usually, each person or team is given a set amount of time to present its case. The participants take turns stating their arguments until the time set aside for the debate is up.

THE ISSUE

In recent years, scientists have documented a general warming of Earth's climate. Many people believe this is due to increased greenhouse gases from the burning of **fossil fuels**. Many developed nations have been reluctant to develop effective plans to deal with climate change. The Inuit fear that one of the long-term effects of ignoring this problem will be the melting of the Arctic Sea ice. Climate change is already endangering many of the animals the Inuit depend upon for food. The Inuit way of life, including their economy, culture, and traditions, is undergoing major changes because of these environmental shifts.

THE QUESTION

Should international agencies and governments immediately develop an aggressive plan to deal with the effects of climate change?

THE SIDES

NO

Developed Nations: Though global temperatures may be warming, it is not certain that this is from human activities. A radical plan to reduce the burning of fossil fuels would hurt the world economy with an uncertain result.

YES

Inuit: Our way of life, our economy, and our culture are linked to the environment. Allowing climate change to continue would be a breach of our human rights.

Ready, Set, Go

Form two teams to debate the issue, and decide whether your team will play the role of the Inuit or the role of the developed nations. Each team should use this book and other research to develop solid arguments for its side and to understand how the issue affects each group. At the end of the role-play debate, discuss how you feel after hearing both points of view.

World Cultures Quiz!

1 How did the ancestors of the Inuit people arrive in North America?

2 What does the word *Inuit* mean?

3 According to Inuit culture, what were the Northern Lights?

4 Who was Sedna?

5 How did the Inuit people develop a written language?

∿	su
∪	lu
∿	ju

6 What might happen if an Inuit hunter did not obey hunting rules and customs?

7 What is the name for a traditional Inuit shelter?

8 How did Inuit women soften an animal hide to use it for clothing?

9 What was the name for Inuit boots?

10 How did the Inuit travel long distances across land or ice?

Key Words

agility the ability to move quickly

ancestors people, plants, animals, and objects from past generations

Arctic large area surrounding the North Pole, where trees do not grow and the ground never fully thaws; the most northern part of the world

banished sent away from a community; forbidden to return to a community

canvas a strong fabric

climate the weather found in a particular area

commercial having to do with business or making money

council a group of people chosen to make decisions for a community

descendants people who come from a particular ancestor

dialects forms of a language spoken in a specific region

dome a rounded roof

driftwood wood that is floating in a body of water or washed on a shore

endangered at risk of disappearing completely

evolved something that has developed gradually

finances to provide money; the way money is managed

fossil fuels fuels, such as coal, oil, or natural gas, made from the ancient remains of plant and animal life

harpoons spear-like tools used for hunting

hide thick animal skin that is used for clothing

indigenous peoples the first settlers to arrive in a particular region

interpreters people whose job it is to explain what someone is saying in another language

intestine a long tube inside the body through which food travels as it is being digested

Inuit a group of indigenous peoples who live in the cold northern regions of Asia, Europe, and North America

kayaks light, narrow boats with coverings over the top

linguists people who know a language very well and study that language

narwhal sinews cords that connect the muscle and bone in a small Arctic whale

nomadic regularly moving from one area to another; never settling in one place

Northern Lights bright-colored beams of light that appear in the sky at night

overharvesting gathering more than is available

preserving keeping something safe or protecting something

spiritual having to do with the spirit; not of the physical world

standardize to make things of the same type with the same features

Index

Log on to www.av2books.com

AV² by Weigl brings you media enhanced books that support active learning. Go to www.av2books.com, and enter the special code found on page 2 of this book. You will gain access to enriched and enhanced content that supplements and complements this book. Content includes video, audio, weblinks, quizzes, a slide show, and activities.

Audio
Listen to sections of the book read aloud.

Video
Watch informative video clips.

Embedded Weblinks
Gain additional information for research.

Try This!
Complete activities and hands-on experiments.

WHAT'S ONLINE?

Try This!	Embedded Weblinks	Video	EXTRA FEATURES
Map the area in which the Inuit live.	Learn more about the Inuit.	Watch a video of Inuit dancing and drumming.	**Audio** Listen to sections of the book read aloud.
Write a biography about a well-known Inuit person.	Read about the history of the Inuit.	See how the Inuit live today.	
Create a timeline showing the history of the Inuit.	View the arts and crafts of the Inuit.		**Key Words** Study vocabulary, and complete a matching word activity.
Draw a chart to show the foods the Inuit eat.			**Slide Show** View images and captions, and prepare a presentation.
Test your knowledge of the Inuit.			**Quizzes** Test your knowledge.

AV² was built to bridge the gap between print and digital. We encourage you to tell us what you like and what you want to see in the future.

Sign up to be an AV² Ambassador at www.av2books.com/ambassador.